This is a book about **CAKE**, all different types of cake. If you like to **EAT** cake or **BAKE** cake, then this is the book for you.

Warning—this book may make you **HUNGRY** . . .

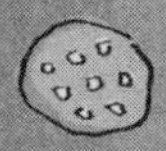

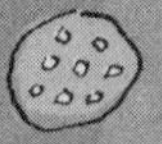

For my god-daughter Marlie—HW

For Amelia, George and Freya—AG

First American Edition 2021
Kane Miller, A Division of EDC Publishing

Freddie's Amazing Bakery: The Cookie Mystery was originally published in English in 2020. This edition is published by arrangement with Oxford University Press.

For information contact:
Kane Miller, A Division of EDC Publishing
5402 S 122nd E Ave, Tulsa, OK 74146
www.kanemiller.com
www.usbornebooksandmore.com

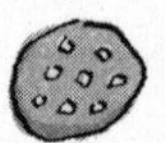

Library of Congress Control Number: 2020936314

Printed and bound in the United States of America
2 3 4 5 6 7 8 9 10

ISBN: 978-1-68464-067-6

WRITTEN BY
HARRIET WHITEHORN

ILLUSTRATED BY
ALEX G. GRIFFITHS

Our story is set in a town called *Belville*—look, here is a map of it. As you can see, it is a delightful place, just the right size, and crisscrossed by a spiderweb of pretty canals (perfect for boating in the summer and skating in the winter), which are lined with cherry trees and tall old houses.

FREDDIE'S AMAZING BAKERY
MACAROON'S PATISSERIE
VAN DE LUNE'S HOTEL
Van de Lune Hotel
MAIN CANAL
NOAH'S CAFÉ

CHAPTER ONE

It was a beautiful spring day in Belville. The sky was a soft, clear blue with a few streaky clouds and the cherry trees along the canals were just bursting into fluffy pink blossoms.

The tables outside Freddie's Amazing Bakery were full of happy people sitting in the sun, eating yummy cakes and pastries, and chatting. And inside the shop, Freddie was putting the finishing touches to a couple of very special cakes. Can you see his French bulldog, Flapjack, looking at the cake? Flapjack was getting excited because he knew it was nearly delivery time, which was his favorite part of the day. He would sit in the basket on the front of Freddie's bicycle while they zoomed all over Belville, delivering cakes.

Now let me introduce you to someone else—Amira, who is Freddie's best friend and manages the shop for him. She was just putting a notice in the window. Can you see what it says?

Amira smiled to herself. She'd always known what an amazing, hardworking baker Freddie was, even when he had no confidence in himself. And now she was very happy because the rest of Belville had realized how amazing he was too. Everyone particularly loved the showstopper cakes that Freddie made on the last Friday of every month. They had turned into a great event—when Freddie put the cake in the shop window, first thing in the morning, all the good people of the town would come and take pictures, saying things like:

"Did you ever see such a FANTASTIC cake?"

and, “Wow! That Freddie really can bake!”

And then, at five o’clock, Amira would auction the cake off to the highest bidder. It was all very exciting! They always gave the money to a charity or good cause and Freddie loved making the showstoppers. He often found his inspiration for them when he was cycling around Belville.

A few minutes after Amira put the job notice up, Freddie came out of the kitchen, carrying a large stack of delivery boxes.

“Freddie, shall I tell anyone who’s interested in the job to come for an interview the day after tomorrow? And bring a cake they’ve made?”

“Yes, good idea,” Freddie said. “I’ve got to dash now, but I’ll see you later.”

“Sure,” Amira replied. “Oh, and I hope it goes well at Van de Lune’s!” she added.

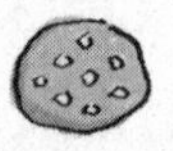

Van de Lune’s was the grandest hotel in Belville and Freddie made all its cakes. And that day he had a particularly important delivery to make there. As you can see from the map at the front of the book, the hotel was a little way away from Freddie’s Amazing Bakery, so Freddie made a few stops en route. All the canals were having street parties to coincide with the cherry blossoms blooming so Freddie was super busy. He delivered . . .

 25 toffee meringues and a large box of assorted éclairs to First Canal

 1 enormous white chocolate cake and 3 quiches to Second Canal

and 30 sausage rolls and 30 custard tarts to Third Canal.

Finally, Freddie drew up in front of Van de Lune's Hotel. Outside, there was a large crowd of people holding up signs and wearing T-shirts saying things like **WE LOVE YOU, COOKIE** and **COOKIE RULES THE WORLD**.

Now, I obviously need to explain to you what that was all about. Two months before there had been a competition on television to find the most beautiful cat in the world and the winner was a cat called Cookie. Cookie became a superstar overnight, with a camera crew filming her every move and her own daily TV show.

She also attracted a whole band of superfans that followed her wherever she went, and that included Van de Lune's Hotel, where she happened to be staying on her way to a cat show. Freddie had made Cookie and her owner a couple of especially delicious cakes.

Freddie parked his bike by the side entrance to the hotel and lifted Flapjack out of his basket. Then he got the two boxes of cakes out of the cart on the back of his bicycle and carried them carefully into the hotel, with Flapjack scampering along behind him. He took the first box to the hotel restaurant as usual and then he went over to take the elevator to the penthouse suite where Cookie was staying.

"Flapjack, I think you should stay down here. Cookie is probably scared of dogs." Flapjack put his head on one side and looked at Freddie with a very serious expression on his face, as if to say, *Don't leave me all alone. I promise to behave.*

"OK then," Freddie relented. "You can come up to the top floor, but you have to wait by the elevator. We don't want to give Cookie a fright."

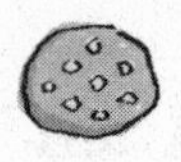

The elevator stopped, the doors opened, and they both walked out, but—oh dear! Who should they come face-to-face with but Cookie herself. She was a gorgeous cream puff of a cat with long, milky colored hair that darkened to chocolate brown around her face and legs, and bright-blue eyes like a doll's. She was on a lead held by a young woman who had bright-red hair, arranged on top of her head a little like a bird's nest, and a friendly, freckly face. She was wearing a flowery dress with big black boots.

"Oh no, I'm so sorry!" Freddie gasped, expecting Cookie to hiss and try to run away. But that didn't happen. Not at all. In fact something remarkable occurred.

Cookie began to purr and came right up to Flapjack and nuzzled him. Flapjack looked rather surprised, but he began to wag his tail.

"Wow!" Freddie said. "Does she always do that with dogs?"

The woman laughed. "Yes, Cookie loves dogs. And they seem to like her too."

"Well she certainly is a remarkable cat," Freddie said. "Let me introduce myself: I'm Freddie and this is my dog, Flapjack."

"Nice to meet you, Freddie. I'm Posy Finkle, Cookie's owner," the young woman replied.

"It's nice to meet you too. Gosh, you must be so proud of Cookie and how famous she is."

Posy nodded, but Freddie thought she

looked a little anxious. "It's fantastic, of course, but I think poor Cookie is feeling the pressure a bit."

At that moment a bossy looking young man brandishing a clipboard came striding into the corridor.

“Posy, we’ll need Cookie back in two minutes for fluff and groom,” he said sharply and then he noticed Flapjack.

“What is that dog doing here?!”

“Oh, he’s fine, Hubert, don’t worry,” Posy replied, nervously. Freddie could see that she was a bit scared of the young man. “Hubert, this is Freddie. And Freddie, this is Hubert. He’s in charge of the TV show . . .”

“. . . And Cookie,” Hubert cut in as he looked Freddie up and down rudely. “And what exactly are you doing here, Freddie?” he asked.

“I’m a baker,” Freddie replied. “I just brought some cakes that I thought Posy and Cookie might enjoy. One is a special cat cake for Cookie made out of tuna and salmon and the other is chocolate with crème and apricot jam, for Posy.”

"Ooh, how delicious! I'm sure we'll both love them," exclaimed Posy. "Thank you so much!"

"Did you say cake?" Hubert queried. "Out of the question. I'm sure Cookie's gaining weight and that is strictly forbidden by the contract."

"But it's made of fish," Freddie explained. "It's all natural ingredients and very healthy."

However, Hubert just wagged his finger and repeated, "No cake. And if you've finished delivering, don't you think you should be on your way?"

He turned to Posy. "And Cookie to fluff and groom in one minute!"

"Er, Hubert, please could Cookie have a bit longer so that I can take her across to the park for just a short time?" Posy asked. "She hasn't been outside for three days."

"Absolutely not," Hubert replied. "We're late as it is. One minute!"

Thankfully, someone called his name and Hubert scurried off.

Poor Cookie! Freddie thought.

"He seemed really nice when we first met him . . ." Posy trailed off with a sigh. "Anyway, thank you for the cakes. I'm sorry that Cookie isn't allowed hers."

"Keep them both anyway," Freddie said, handing her the boxes. "You never know, you might be able to give it to her later."

Posy smiled. "We'd better go, but it was so nice to meet you, Freddie, and you too, Flapjack. Hopefully we'll see you again soon."

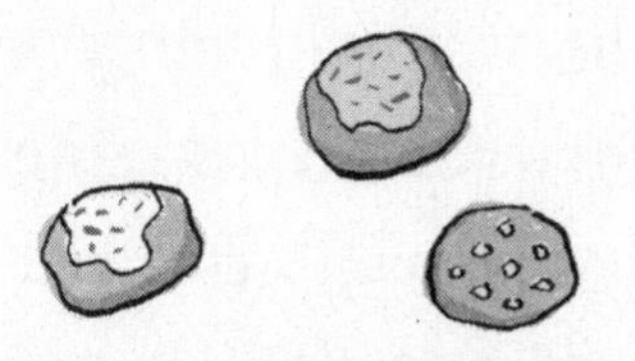

CHAPTER TWO

And now it's time for you to meet someone else—Bernard Macaroon, owner of Macaroon's Patisserie and his rather horrible cat, Otto.

Now what you really need to know about Bernard is that he was one of those annoying people who have to be the best at everything. I'm sure you know someone like that, don't you? And if Bernard wasn't on top, he got really, really cross. So, of course, he was incredibly jealous of Freddie and what an amazing baker he was. Funnily enough, Bernard came from a long line of excellent bakers, but sadly he hadn't inherited their talent. What he was good at was measuring things, very precisely, and so he always just stuck to their old recipes and never tried anything new. As a result of this his cakes were OK, but a bit on the dull side.

That morning, Bernard was feeling particularly poisonous toward Freddie for two reasons. First of all, his beloved sports car had broken down and when he had taken it to the garage, the mechanics were all eating a chocolate birthday cake from

Freddie's and going on and on about how delicious it was, much to Bernard's fury.

Then he had been to the dentist's. The dentist had told him off for eating too many sweet things and given him two fillings, which was bad enough in itself, but then, just as he was drilling into Bernard's teeth, the dentist started telling Bernard how much he adored Freddie's cakes, and weren't they just scrumptious, particularly the macarons. This made Bernard feel **SO CROSS** that if it hadn't been for the fact that the dentist was drilling he would have had a **MASSIVE** tantrum.

So now Bernard was walking home, thinking bad thoughts about Freddie and his blasted cakes. Otto was waddling along next to him, thinking equally bad thoughts about all the birds tweeting in the spring sunshine in the trees and how much he'd like to chase them. As they passed Van de Lune's Hotel, Bernard saw Freddie's bike, with all the boxes of cakes ready to be delivered in the back, and he felt like it must be a sign. After checking that there was no one around, Bernard trotted over to the bike.

What Bernard really wanted to do was to put all the boxes on the ground and jump up and down on them, a bit like when you are ruining a sandcastle on the beach. But what he actually decided to do was much more cunning and, Bernard thought, very clever indeed.

"I'm going to try one of Freddie's cakes instead," he decided. "I'm sure it won't be nearly as good as mine, but if it is a tiny bit better then I'll be able to work out why it is, and then make my cakes **THE BEST!**"

Bernard grinned to himself as he picked up the top box and lifted its lid. There, nestled like jewels, was a selection of Freddie's scrumptious looking macarons.

Bernard's mouth began to water, and his hand darted to a raspberry-colored one and shoved it in his mouth.

You know when you bite into something and you just cannot believe how delicious it is? Bernard's mouth was filled with the most luscious mixture of creamy raspberry filling and soft but chewy, yummy, fruity macaron. He couldn't help but let out a moan of pleasure as he reached for another, and then another and then . . . well, you know what happened. Bernard ate the whole box of macarons!

Those are so good, thought Bernard. *I've got to work out how Freddie does it.*

But his thoughts were interrupted by a noise from nearby and Bernard could see Flapjack bounding out of the side door. He dropped the empty box, grabbed the full ones, and sped off, with Otto lumbering behind him. Flapjack saw them before they disappeared around a corner. He ran after the pair, barking furiously.

"Flapjack! What are you doing?" Freddie called, as he came out of the hotel a moment later and saw the dog speeding off.

That's strange, Freddie thought and then he noticed the empty cardboard box on the ground and the missing boxes.

"Oh no!" he cried. "Someone has stolen all my cakes!"

"Flapjack!" he called again and this time Flapjack came running back, looking cross. He barked at Freddie as if to say, *They got away!*

"I know," Freddie replied with a

sigh. "Never mind. We'd better go and tell the police about the theft and then go back to the bakery and get some more cakes." He looked at the empty box that Bernard had discarded. "I'll take this just in case the thief left any fingerprints," he said and picked it up off the ground. And then he lifted Flapjack into the front basket and set off.

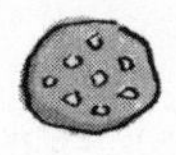

Meanwhile, Bernard and Otto had made it back to Macaroon's Patisserie. Bernard plonked the boxes of cakes down in his office, got out a notebook and pen, and took a bite of one of Freddie's strawberry cheesecakes.

Just like the macarons, it was absolutely yummy. Bernard tried to work out what he was tasting—plump, sweet strawberries, obviously, but was there a slight tang of lemon? Then came the dense, creamy filling, but could he also taste orange? Bernard wondered. And the biscuit base—how did he get it so crunchy? There was a gingery taste to it. Or was it nutmeg?

Bernard couldn't figure it out, so he took another bite, but this time the topping seemed to taste more of orange than lemon, and the creamy section of toffee, and then the base of honey. But how much? A drop . . . a teaspoon . . . two teaspoons? Bernard was a baker who needed exact measurements and his mind was whizzing faster than an electric whisk! Just when he thought he might **EXPLODE** from all the questions, he was interrupted by a knock at the door.

"Yes?!" he shouted grumpily.

The door opened and one of his assistants, Sophie, came in. Sophie was small, softly spoken, with neat blonde hair and curious hazel eyes.

"Sorry to bother you, Bernard, but I was just going to tell you that we've run out of flour. The delivery didn't come today and . . ."

"Oh never mind that now," Bernard interrupted her. "I need your help."

Sophie raised her eyebrows in surprise because Bernard never normally asked for her help. And then, as she approached his desk, she was doubly surprised to see the boxes from Freddie's bakery, as she knew how much her boss hated Freddie. Sophie, on the other hand, really admired Freddie and she often stopped in at Freddie's Amazing Bakery on her way home to buy something for her supper. But she knew better than to ever mention this to Bernard.

"Try this cheesecake," he ordered Sophie. "And tell me what flavors you can taste."

Sophie did as she was told. After a few

moments of delicate chewing, she said, "Elderflower cordial with the strawberries and then there is a touch of vanilla in the cheese part and cinnamon and very dark brown sugar in the biscuit base."

Bernard nodded.

"Yes, that's just what I thought," he lied. "The question, though, is how much of each? I must have exact measurements."

Sophie raised her eyebrows again.

"Are you going to . . ." she paused as she had been going to say "copy" but wondered if it sounded a bit rude. "Are you going to do something similar?"

"Possibly," Bernard blustered. "But much better, obviously. Now, do you want to help me?"

Sophie, who was a really good baker, had been trying to get Bernard to make his cakes and pastries more interesting since she had started to work for him, but he got so cross every time she mentioned it that she had given up. So she was pleased to hear what Bernard was saying.

"Of course!" she replied. "Let's try the other cakes and see if we can work some of Freddie's magic on ours," and then when she saw Bernard's scowl, she quickly added, "I mean let's take his best ideas and make them much, much better."

Bernard's face relaxed like a pan of boiling milk when you take it off the stove.

"Thank you, Sophie," he replied and then added grandly, "Report back to me the day after tomorrow. And if I'm pleased with your work, you can go on that patisserie course in Paris that you are so keen on."

Sophie gasped with excitement.

"You'd give me a whole two weeks off in August to go to study at the École Pâtissier?" she said.

"Of course," Bernard replied, thinking he could always change his mind if he decided it didn't suit him.

"Thank you so much!" Sophie cried, practically skipping out of the door.

CHAPTER THREE

The following day Freddie got up very early as usual—bakers always have to get up early—and after doing his kung fu practice and feeding Flapjack, he went down his baker's chute to the kitchen to begin baking. Amira arrived shortly after. She was clutching a copy of the *Belville News*.

"You'll never guess what has happened!" she gasped. "Cookie has gone missing, presumed stolen!"

"No!" Freddie exclaimed and looked at the newspaper headlines with her.

THE *Belville* NEWS

SUPERSTAR CAT DISAPPEARS FROM LUXURY HOTEL

"That's awful!" Freddie said. "Posy, her owner, must be so upset."

"The police say that they think Cookie may have been kidnapped," Amira said. "And they're waiting for a ransom demand."

Freddie glanced down at Flapjack. He

couldn't think of anything worse than someone taking his little friend.

Just at that moment, the telephone rang.

"That's very early for a customer," Freddie remarked, and he answered it saying, "Freddie's Amazing Bakery, Freddie speaking."

"Hello, it's Inspector Brown here, from the police."

"Good morning, Inspector. How can I help you?"

"I wanted to ask you a few more questions about your stolen cakes, to see if there is any connection with Cookie's disappearance."

"Of course, anything to help find Cookie," Freddie replied. "I can pop into the station this afternoon while I'm on my deliveries, if that suits you?"

"That should be fine. Thank you, Freddie," the Inspector said and hung up.

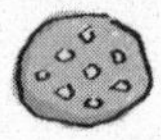

Freddie explained the conversation to Amira, who said, "Gosh, I wonder if it was the same person?" Then she glanced at the kitchen clock and exclaimed, "Goodness, we'd better get on. I've got a stack of bills to pay before we open."

"It's going to be a very busy morning," said Freddie, checking the order list for that day. "By the way, did anyone ask about the job?" he added.

"Yes! I'm sorry, all this Cookie business knocked it right out of my head," Amira replied. "Eight people want to apply!"

"Wow!" gasped Freddie. "So many!"

"I know," said Amira. "I think

we'll have to shut the shop tomorrow afternoon to see them all."

Freddie thought for a moment. "Yes, if I get up super early and then really rush the deliveries I can probably be back by two."

"Perfect," said Amira.

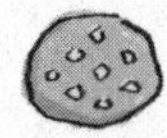

Freddie had a very busy morning of baking and then leapt on his bike to make his deliveries. His first stop was the café in the park.

It was a lovely sunny day and the park was full of children playing, dog walkers walking, and people just enjoying the sunshine. Freddie cycled past the carousel on his way to the café. Usually it was twirling around merrily, its horses gliding up and down to the sound of a jolly tune and giggling children, but that day it was silent and still. *It must be broken,* Freddie thought. *That's a shame on such a sunny day.*

The café was run by Freddie's good friend Noah. Freddie saw Noah a lot, not only because Freddie made all the cakes for the café and delivered them twice a week, but also because they went to kung fu classes together on Wednesday and Friday evenings. Noah had another hobby as well as kung fu and that was bird-watching, and last winter, Freddie had helped him put up lots of bird boxes in the cherry trees around the park. As Freddie cycled along that afternoon under the trees he could hear by all the tweeting and chirping that the boxes had been a great success.

Noah was outside the café pinning up some posters. They said:

"Hi, Freddie," Noah greeted him with a smile.

"Hello, Noah. What's the matter with the carousel?" Freddie asked.

"It stopped suddenly last Friday. The lady who repairs it came yesterday and told me that it needs a new, very expensive, part. I thought I'd try to raise some funds by having a picnic."

"That's a brilliant idea," Freddie said. "Do you want me to make some cakes and sausage rolls for it?"

"That would be great," Noah replied.

Freddie unloaded his cakes and they carried on chatting for a few more minutes before Freddie suddenly noticed that Flapjack was missing.

"I'm sure he won't have gone far," Noah reassured him, looking around.

They began to search for him, calling:

"FLAPJACK!"

"FLAPJACK!"

"It's not like him," Freddie said. "How strange."

A couple more minutes passed and Freddie was beginning to get even more concerned as he remembered what had happened to poor Cookie.

"Here he is!" Noah cried, seeing Flapjack bounding back toward them. "Off on an adventure, eh boy?"

Flapjack gave him a friendly bark.

Freddie was less impressed.

"You mustn't run off like that, Flapjack. I was getting worried." And with that, he lifted him into the bicycle basket, said goodbye to Noah, and cycled on his way.

PICNIC
IN THE
PARK
SATURDAY 15th APRIL
£1 ENTRANCE FEE TO HELP PAY FOR
THE CAROUSEL REPAIRS
Noa

CHAPTER FOUR

Freddie's next stop was the police station. It was very near the park on Flower Canal. Freddie parked his bike outside, and as he lifted Flapjack out of his basket, he said, "No dogs allowed inside I'm afraid, so you be a good boy and stay by the bike, and make sure no one steals anything this time." But do you know what? As soon as Freddie had gone inside, that cheeky dog scampered off again.

And who should walk past a few minutes later? None other than Bernard, with Otto by his side on a lead. They were both scowling, Otto because Bernard had put him on a lead, which he felt was undignified for a cat and also it stopped him chasing birds, and Bernard for four particular reasons:

1 All his staff, with the exception of Sophie, had come to him that morning saying that they simply had to take the afternoon off the following day for a whole range of incredibly important reasons such as attending their great-aunt's funeral, or going to an urgent dental appointment. They were in fact all going to Freddie's for a job interview, but luckily Bernard didn't know this—if he had he would have been **VERY ANGRY INDEED**.

2. Although you would never think of Bernard as softhearted, he was where Otto was concerned. And so the news of Cookie's possible cat-napping had upset him, which was why Otto was now on a lead.

3. It was going to cost a lot of money to have his car repaired.

4. And lastly, the main reason. Bernard simply couldn't get the **DELICIOUS** tastes of Freddie's cakes out of his mind and mouth. He had spent the whole day fantasizing about them and had almost had to send one of his staff out to buy him some cakes. So when he saw Freddie's bicycle propped against the wall, he found his feet stopping.

Then, with barely a second thought, Bernard opened the top box on the cart and took out one of Freddie's chocolate cakes and began to stuff it in his mouth. But in that instant two things happened at once . . .

The first was that Flapjack returned and, seeing what Bernard was up to, began barking fiercely at him.

"Go away!" Bernard shouted at him. But his mouth was so full of chocolate cake that it came out as "BOW BUBAY!"

Otto puffed himself up and had a jolly good hiss at Flapjack too.

And then a voice behind Bernard said, "Is everything all right?"

He spun around to find Inspector Brown standing before him.

"Yes, yes of course," Bernard replied, trying not to spray him with chocolate cake crumbs as he struggled to swallow the last of it. "Sorry, just having a little snack," he said.

As Flapjack continued to bark at him, the Inspector eyed Bernard a little suspiciously.

"Flapjack seems upset with you," he said.

Bernard decided attack was the best form of defense.

"I know, he's such a vicious dog! Look at him trying to attack my poor Otto!"

Bernard cried.

Inspector Brown replied, "Flapjack seems upset with you, not Otto. And I always think what a nice dog Flapjack is."

Bernard made a harrumphing noise and decided to change the subject.

"So, Inspector, have you caught the catnapper? It is such a terrible thought that someone might steal my Otto."

The Inspector was about to reply when Freddie appeared from the police station.

"Ah, hello, Freddie," the Inspector said. "Sorry I'm late—since Cookie was stolen, it seems that every cat in Belville is being reported missing. Luckily they've all been false alarms so far."

"No problem," Freddie replied cheerily. "What else can I tell you about the theft?" Freddie turned to Bernard and explained. "When I left my bicycle outside Van de Lune's Hotel yesterday, several boxes of cakes were stolen from the trailer."

Flapjack began to bark at Bernard again, but Freddie shushed him.

"Really!" Bernard exclaimed, going rather green and wiping his mouth hurriedly in case there were any smears of chocolate cake still around it. He then looked at his watch very deliberately and said, "Oh dear! Is that the time, I really must be going. Come on, Otto!" And he hurried off.

Flapjack began to follow him, barking, but Freddie called, "Flapjack! Come back now! And stop barking at Bernard. Honestly, Flapjack, what is up with you?"

They both looked at Flapjack, who stared back at them meaningfully.

"He looks like he's trying to tell us something, doesn't he?" the Inspector said. "If only dogs could talk, eh? I'm sure they could tell us a great deal."

Freddie smiled.

"Yes and mostly about food," he replied. "So did the cake box have any fingerprints on it?"

"It did, but they were very smudged. I've sent it away for further testing. We should get the results at the weekend."

"Have you got any other leads in the Cookie case?" Freddie asked.

The Inspector sighed.

"Not really," he said. "We don't know at this stage if Cookie's been kidnapped or stolen. All that is certain is that Posy left the window open onto the fire escape, so whoever took Cookie came in and left that way."

"Poor Posy," Freddie said.

"I know," the Inspector said. "She's beside herself. And all the Cookie fans weeping and wailing outside the hotel don't help. Anyway, thanks for talking to me, Freddie, and see you soon."

"It's a pleasure—I only hope that you find Cookie soon. Bye and good luck."

"Bye, Freddie," the Inspector said and went into the police station.

CHAPTER FIVE

The following day, Freddie got up even earlier than usual, and galloped through his baking and deliveries at top speed so that by 1:30 p.m. he only had one more delivery to make. It wasn't strictly on his list, but it was something that had been on his mind since seeing Inspector Brown the day before. He stopped to buy a bunch of flowers and then took them, along with a small box of cakes, to the top of Van de Lune's Hotel. Flapjack went with him.

Posy Finkle was sitting in the suite, which looked large and empty. Hubert and all the TV cameras had left since they had nothing to film without Cookie.

"I'm so sorry about Cookie," Freddie said, handing her the flowers. "And I brought you some cakes just in case you felt like eating something."

"Thank you, you're very kind. And here's your sweet dog," she said stroking Flapjack. "I miss Cookie so much," Posy said, her eyes filling with tears. "And

I feel so guilty—it was me who made her famous by entering her in the competition in the first place. And then I left the window open—it was just so stuffy in here—and now she's gone! It's all my fault she's been stolen."

"You mustn't be so hard on yourself, Posy," said Freddie. "None of it's your fault. And I'm sure the police will have some news for you very soon."

Posy nodded, trying to smile.

"There's a picnic in the park at the weekend," Freddie continued. "Why don't you come along? It might cheer you up."

"You're very kind, Freddie. Thank you. I might."

"Good," Freddie said. "I'd better get going, but hopefully we'll see you on Saturday."

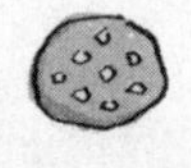

When Freddie returned to the bakery, Amira was waiting for him. "Just in time," she said. "The first job applicant has arrived. I hope you're hungry because you're going to have to try eight cakes this afternoon!"

"Yikes," Freddie replied with a laugh. "I can't believe that so many people want to work here."

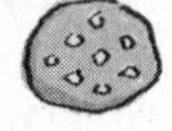

Meanwhile, over at Macaroon's Patisserie, Sophie was all alone in the kitchen and putting the final touches to some cakes and quiches that she had made for Bernard to try . . .

Much as Sophie would love to work at Freddie's, she had decided not to apply for the job in case Bernard found out and decided not to give her the raise and let her go to Paris. It had always been Sophie's dream to study at the famous École Pâtissier, so she couldn't risk losing the chance now. She had stayed up all the previous night making batch after batch of the cakes and quiches until they were perfect. She had been rushed off her feet over lunchtime, covering for everyone else, but by the middle of the afternoon the patisserie was quiet, so she knocked on Bernard's office door.

Bernard was **FUMING**. He had just discovered where all his staff really were that afternoon and so his hatred of Freddie had now been turned up to **FULL VOLUME**. He was pacing up and down his room, ranting to Otto about his disloyal staff and how sneaky and two-faced Freddie was, trying to steal all his staff. So it probably wasn't the best time for Sophie to come into his office and say, "Hi, Bernard. I've spent the last couple of days working on some cakes and pastries which are a bit more like Freddie's. They're not as good, obviously, but I think they're a start. So here's a quiche made with leeks, bacon, and lots of herbs, and also a lemon cake. Do you want to try them and I can explain all the flavors I've used for you? I've written down the quantities very precisely."

Bernard felt himself go very hot and then very cold with anger.

"How dare you mention that boy's name to me?"

he hissed at her.

Sophie was a bit scared because she could see how cross Bernard was, but she was determined not to be bullied by him so she said bravely, "But we agreed that I would do this when we tried some of Freddie's cakes together—remember?"

"I don't care!" Bernard shouted, like a furious toddler. "I never want to hear that name again. And you can take your disgusting quiche and cakes and throw them in the trash!"

And, as if that wasn't bad enough, Bernard took Sophie's quiche and threw it on the floor, breaking the plate. He was about to do the same with the cake, but Sophie shouted,

"STOP!"

very loudly at him.

Bernard did stop. He looked at her as she scooped up the quiche from the floor and picked up the plate with her cake on it and walked out of the door, without saying a word. She put the cake down in the kitchen and then took the quiche straight out to the trash cans, at the back of the shop.

Otto was often to be found lurking by the trash cans, waiting to pounce on some poor mouse or rat trying to grab a few crumbs. However, when Sophie went outside today, he wasn't there. But someone else was . . .

"Hello, Flapjack," Sophie said, surprised. She looked around for Freddie, but there was no sign of him. *Of course*, she remembered, *he'll be busy interviewing*. "What are you up to?"

Flapjack gave her a bark and looked

longingly at the quiche.

"Really, Flapjack?" Sophie queried. "I'm sure you get plenty of food at home."

But then he made a mewling noise at her, put his head on one side, and generally looked so adorable that she gave in.

"Oh, OK then," she said, and gave him a little bit, putting the rest in the trash. "I think I should take you home," Sophie went on. "I'm sure you're not supposed to be wandering around alone." And she was about to grab him when a voice bellowed,

"WHAT ARE YOU DOING GIVING THAT VICIOUS DOG FOOD?"

Sophie turned around to find Bernard **GLOWERING** at her. In a rare moment of compassion he had been feeling slightly guilty about how he had spoken to Sophie, and had actually come out to apologize to her. But the sight of her giving food to Freddie's dog was too much for him. Flapjack took one look at Bernard and sped away.

"Well, you clearly didn't want it, so someone else might as well have it," Sophie replied sharply. She was doubly cross with Bernard now, not only for shouting at her, but also for scaring Flapjack away. "And I've never known Flapjack to be vicious—unlike some other animals I could mention," Sophie said, looking at Otto, who had followed Bernard out into the back alley.

"How dare you insult Otto and me!"

Bernard cried, and then in a moment of madness bellowed,

"That's it! I never want to see you again.

You are **FIRED!**"

Sophie gasped. She could feel her eyes filling with tears, but she said calmly, "Fine. I'll just get my things and go." And she walked back in, ripped off her apron, and put on her coat. Then she picked up her cake and marched out of the patisserie.

CHAPTER SIX

Sophie's route took her past Freddie's and she saw Amira and Freddie talking alone inside the shop. *The interviews must have finished,* she thought with a sigh. *I'm so silly for thinking things would work out with Bernard; I should have just tried for the job at Freddie's like everyone else.*

She was about to walk on when she remembered Flapjack. *I should go and check if he got home* OK, she thought and opened the shop door.

"Sorry to bother you," Sophie began.

"Sophie!" Amira cried. "Come in. I was hoping we would see you this afternoon. Freddie, you know Sophie, don't you? She comes in the shop sometimes—she works for Bernard."

"I did work for him," Sophie replied, her voice a little sad and shaky, "but he just fired me."

"Oh no, I'm so sorry!" said Amira.

"Have you come for an interview here?" Freddie asked, kindly. "I see you brought a cake."

"Aren't I too late?" Sophie asked.

"Not at all," Freddie replied.

Sophie smiled. "Oh, yes please, then. But first I must tell you that I saw Flapjack earlier, at the back of Bernard's shop."

"Really!" Freddie exclaimed and he

looked through the open door to the kitchen where Flapjack was curled up in his basket. "What's this I hear, Flapjack? You were at Bernard's?" he said. Flapjack opened one eye and, seeing Sophie, hastily shut it and pretended to be asleep.

"Honestly, he's such a monkey at the moment," Freddie said with a sigh.

"Oh well, I'm just pleased he's come

home," Sophie said.

"Shall we try your cake?" Amira said. "It looks delicious."

Sophie smiled as Amira cut herself and Freddie slices of her lemon cake.

After a moment's chewing, Freddie said, "That's absolutely delicious. Did you put rosemary in it?"

"Yes," Sophie replied. "I really like the two flavors together."

"It's outstanding," Amira announced, helping herself to another slice.

"Sophie, that's by far the best cake we've tasted this afternoon," Freddie said.

"Definitely," Amira agreed.

They exchanged glances and then Freddie said, "Sophie, would you consider coming to work here? As my assistant?"

Sophie's face lit up like a light bulb. "I would love that."

"Excellent. We couldn't pay you a huge amount, but I would teach you everything I know," Freddie said.

"That would be fantastic," Sophie replied, thinking about the patisserie course in Paris.

"Is there something else?" Amira asked, seeing Sophie hesitate. "It's OK to ask, we don't bite!" she joked.

Sophie smiled and said, "It's always been my dream to study at the École Pâtissier in Paris and there is a two-week course in August. Would it be possible for me to go one year?"

"Of course," Freddie replied. "You can go this year—it's a great thing for you to do and we are so quiet in August that it would be absolutely fine."

"Thank you," Sophie said, beaming.

"Do you think you can start

tomorrow?" Freddie asked. "We've got to begin the baking for the picnic in the park on Saturday."

"Absolutely," Sophie replied with delight.

Well that's all worked out rather well, hasn't it? News of Sophie's new job traveled fast and by the afternoon of the following day, Bernard had heard. And oh dear! He wasn't happy. Not at all. And his imagination started going into overdrive.

"I bet she was working for Freddie the whole time," Bernard ranted at Otto. "Spying on me, stealing my best ideas, and sabotaging my cakes! That's why everyone thinks Freddie's cakes are better than mine—Sophie has been ruining everything here! I'm going to go over to Freddie's and give them both a piece of my mind."

Bernard stormed into Freddie's Amazing Bakery ready for battle. The crowd of people in the shop, the delicious smells wafting around, and the displays of mouthwatering cakes and pastries only maddened him further. Amira was behind the counter, and just as Bernard opened his mouth to start shouting at her, something happened. Something extraordinary.

Bernard had Otto with him as usual and he had picked the cat up, holding him under one arm. When Amira saw Otto, with his grumpy squished-up face, she couldn't help but smile and she leaned over and stroked him. Unusually Otto began to purr . . . and Bernard, well, he felt very strange indeed. He looked at Amira and realized he'd never really noticed her smooth skin, swooshy hair, and large brown eyes before. He felt a strange fluttering in his chest and all his anger disappeared like air rushing out of a burst balloon, to be replaced by something else, soft and squishy like cotton balls. When she smiled at him, and asked if she could help, he just stared at her.

"Can I help you, Bernard?" she repeated.

"Er . . . yes . . . sorry . . ." he stammered. "Hello, Amira. How absolutely lovely to see you again."

"And you, Bernard," Amira replied, trying not to sound too surprised at Bernard's sudden friendliness. "How can I help?"

"Is Freddie around?" Bernard asked casually.

"No, I'm afraid not—he's out on his deliveries," said Amira. "Was it something I can deal with instead?"

"No, no, don't worry," Bernard replied quickly. He knew he should go, but he found he couldn't quite bear to leave Amira yet. So he grinned foolishly at her, and said, "Actually you can help me. Please can I buy one of your a-mazing chocolate cakes?"

"Of course, I'll just put it in a box for you."

"Thank you so much," Bernard gushed.

"Is there anything else?" Amira asked gently after she had handed him the box and he had given her some money—because he was still standing there!

"Er no . . . er yes, actually. Is Sophie working here?"

Amira looked concerned. "She started this morning. She's in the kitchen. There's not a problem is there, Bernard? She said she had lost her job with you . . ."

"No, no problem at all," Bernard said hurriedly, in case he upset Amira in any way. "I'm just so pleased that she has found another job."

He gave her another large, cheesy grin.

"Well, we're delighted to have her.

We're really busy making all the cakes for the street parties and then the picnic in the park this weekend."

"Will you be going?" Bernard asked eagerly.

"Yes, I think so," Amira replied.

"Fantastic!" said Bernard in a very un-Bernard type way. "I'll see you there. Goodbye, Amira!"

"Bye, Bernard," Amira replied. As she watched him walk back across the square she slowly shook her head. "Well that was all a bit strange . . ." she murmured to herself.

CHAPTER SEVEN

Freddie arrived back later in a terrible fluster. Flapjack had run off again while he was doing his deliveries.

"I just let him out of his basket for a few minutes while I was taking some cakes into the museum. When I came out again he was gone."

"Don't worry," Amira replied calmly, "I'm sure he'll be back soon."

Freddie nodded and tried to distract himself by thinking of ideas for his next showstopper cake. But it was no good; after about twenty minutes, he announced:

"I think I'd better ring Inspector Brown and report him missing."

As Freddie went to pick up the phone, Posy came into the shop with a shamefaced Flapjack on a lead made out of a piece of string.

"Oh, thank you so much, Posy! Where did you find him?" Freddie cried.

"In the market, by the bread stall," Posy replied.

"He wasn't trying to beg for food was he?" Freddie asked.

"Er, yes, I'm afraid he was," said Posy.

"Flapjack!" said Freddie, turning to the little dog, who was looking a bit sheepish. "What is the matter with you? Go and get in your basket!" Flapjack scuttled off.

"Is there any news about Cookie?" Freddie asked Posy.

She shook her head sadly.

"No. I would even be grateful for a ransom note now, just to know that she's alive."

"It must be terrible for you," Freddie said.

"I thought I'd hand out some of

these pictures of Cookie at the picnic tomorrow," Posy said, fishing a piece of paper out of her pocket and showing it to the others. There was a photo of Cookie and underneath it said:

"That's a good idea," said Amira. "Hopefully someone will have seen her or remember something about the night she was stolen." Posy paused sadly and then forced herself to be more cheerful. "Anyway, I just wanted to check that Flapjack got back safely. I should be getting along now, so see you at the picnic!"

"See you there!" Freddie and Amira chorused as Posy went off, and then Freddie called after her, "And thank you again!!"

After Posy had gone, Freddie said to Amira, "I just don't understand what Flapjack is up to. He gets enough to eat here—he never used to be so greedy."

"Why don't you take him to Dr. Wells, the vet?" Amira suggested. "He's always really helpful."

"Thanks, Amira, that's a great idea."

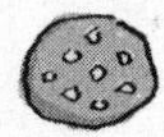

Dr. Wells was a very nice, sensible man with neat brown hair and square spectacles.

Freddie explained the problem with Flapjack, and Dr. Wells said, "How strange. Let's have a look at him then."

Freddie lifted Flapjack up onto the examining table and Dr. Wells carefully checked him over. He weighed him, measured him, listened to his heart, and felt his stomach.

"I'm pleased to say he is in perfect physical health. He's neither too fat nor too thin."

"Well that's good news, obviously," Freddie said. "But it doesn't help me work out why he keeps running away."

Dr. Wells thought for a while before saying, "Why don't you follow him the next time he runs off? And then you can see what he's up to."

"That's a good idea," Freddie said. "I'll give it a try."

Freddie asked Amira and Sophie to help and they made a plan together. They would keep a very close eye on Flapjack all afternoon until about six o'clock. By then the shop would be quieting down. Then they would all pretend to be very busy and not be paying Flapjack any attention, and Sophie would "accidentally" leave the back door open. And when Flapjack ran off, Amira and Freddie would follow him while Sophie looked after the shop.

The plan worked like magic at first. No sooner had Sophie left the door open than she saw, out of the corner of her eye, Flapjack sneak out. She dashed into the shop and whispered to the others, "He's gone!" and Amira and Freddie sprinted after him.

It all started well—they followed Flapjack as he charged across the square and down Window Canal. They watched as he made a quick detour to the back of Macaroon's Patisserie, but then, because Bernard was outside, he swerved off and headed over to Main Canal. He stopped outside the butcher's shop, but the butcher shooed him away. Off he went to the fishmongers on Flower Canal, where he scooted around the back. Someone had just put out their trash and Flapjack carefully extracted a fish from one of the garbage cans and, holding it in his mouth, scampered off.

He then ran up Water Lane and turned into Magnolia Canal. But there things got a bit tricky because the residents of Magnolia Canal were having their street party that evening and it was crowded with people. Freddie and Amira ducked and dived as best they could, but they lost him.

Freddie sighed. “That is so annoying.”

“Well, let’s think logically,” said Amira. “The park is at the other end of Magnolia Canal and then beyond that is the museum.”

“He did go off by the museum earlier today,” Freddie pointed out. “Let’s go down there and see if we can see him.”

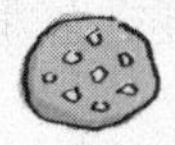

They made their way past the park and down to the museum, but there was no sign of Flapjack.

“Oh dear. I hope he’s not in any danger,” Freddie fretted.

“He won’t be,” Amira said reassuringly. “He’ll probably be back at the bakery by the time we return.”

And sure enough, when they pushed the door open to the bakery, Sophie said with a smile, "Flapjack's in his basket. He came back about five minutes ago."

CHAPTER EIGHT

The day of the picnic dawned bright and clear. Sophie and Freddie got up very, very early to make all the extra cakes, pastries, sausage rolls, and quiches. Saturdays were the busiest day in the bakery, and doubly so that morning as everyone knew that Freddie was shutting at lunchtime to go to the picnic. Amira was rushed off her feet, but whenever she did have a spare moment, she lent a hand packing everything up to take over to the park. They all worked really hard and by eleven thirty everything was done.

Noah had also been very busy. There was bunting everywhere and a sea of blankets spread out over the grass by the café and a forest of deck chairs around the bandstand. The band had just arrived—the Belville Blasters—and they were busy setting up. There were long trestle tables with large jugs of juice and water and cups for everyone, and lots of yummy party food like spicy chicken, burgers, and pizza.

The
Belville

Amira, Freddie, Sophie, and Noah set out everything from the bakery just as people were beginning to arrive. It looked like it was going to be a marvelous afternoon.

Inspector Brown and Posy Finkle arrived together. Posy was wearing a bright, flowery dress and some sparkly earrings, but Freddie still thought that she was looking very sad. She was holding a large pile of the pictures of Cookie, ready to hand out.

At that moment Bernard drove up in his sports car. He'd just picked it up from the garage and was feeling uncharacteristically happy. He was also dressed in a very un-Bernard type way, in a bright-yellow linen suit, with a green spotted bow tie and handkerchief, and a panama hat. Otto was sitting in the passenger seat, wearing a matching green spotted bow tie. On the back seat was a large bunch of tulips.

"Good morning!" said Bernard in such a friendly tone that Freddie and the Inspector looked amazed. He beamed at all of them as he got out of his car and then turned his attention to Amira. He looked at her, his brown eyes large and puppylike, and he went a little pink, as he said, "I hope you don't mind, I brought these for you." And he presented her with the tulips.

Amira smiled politely and took them.

"That's very kind of you, Bernard—thank you so much," she said, making him go even pinker.

"What a sweet cat!" Posy said, bending down to stroke Otto. But Otto hissed and lunged at her hand, teeth bared.

"Oh!" Posy cried and pulled her hand back quickly.

"What are you doing startling him like that!" Bernard snapped and then, remembering that he was trying to impress Amira, quickly added, "I mean, I'm so sorry. He always gets a little nervous around dogs—particularly a cat hater like Flapjack."

"Really?" replied Posy. "I am surprised. Flapjack couldn't have been *sweeter* with Cookie."

Bernard's eyes narrowed and he was about to blurt out a rude reply, but he stopped himself just in time. "I think I will get a drink and go and listen to the band—would you care to join me?" he asked Amira.

"I'm sorry, Bernard, but I'm too busy helping Noah and Freddie. But have a great time," she said and tried to ignore Bernard's sad expression.

"Someone's got a crush on you," Noah teased her after Bernard had left.

"Oh, don't be so silly," Amira replied.

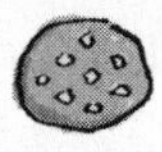

The next couple of hours passed in a delightful picnic-y type way. Everyone ate piles of delicious food and sat around chatting, or snoozing in the sunshine, or playing games. It was just a shame, everyone remarked, that the carousel was still broken.

Suddenly, Bernard came running through the park to Freddie and the others, looking very worried.

"Have you seen Otto?" he asked breathlessly.

"No," they all replied, shaking their heads.

"Didn't you have him on a lead?" Amira asked.

"Yes, but then I took him off it in a moment of madness," Bernard said melodramatically. "He's so devoted to me that he never usually leaves my side. Something MUST have happened to him." He looked accusingly at Flapjack. "Are you sure your dog hasn't been chasing him?"

"I'm positive," Freddie replied. "Flapjack has been here all the time with me."

"Oh no! Do you think the catnapper has struck again?" Posy asked.

Bernard went white at the thought.

"He is an exceptionally beautiful cat with a fine pedigree," Bernard said.

"Really!?" the Inspector said, thinking of Otto's squished-up, grumpy face and low-hanging tummy. "He's probably just wandered off you know—cats do."

"He is everything to me, my Otto, I

cannot bear to lose him," Bernard sobbed, his eyes filling up with tears.

Everyone felt very sorry for Bernard.

"Don't worry, we'll find him," Noah said kindly and got out a loudspeaker from under the table. He took it over to the bandstand, and the band stopped playing while he made an announcement.

"Ladies and gentlemen, boys and girls, I hope you are all having a great time. Unfortunately we have another missing cat, so could everyone please take a few minutes to help us look for him? If we all work together I'm sure we'll find him in no time. His name is Otto and he's a tabby cat, quite . . . er . . . large and wearing a green spotted bow tie."

Everyone began to search, calling, "*Otto!*" and, "*Here, kitty, kitty!*"

"Where's Otto, Flapjack?" Freddie asked, as he searched under the deck chairs and trestle tables. Flapjack bounded off toward the cherry trees, returning just a few minutes later with something in his mouth.

"What's that?" Freddie asked, bending down and pulling it out.

It was a green spotted bow tie.

Bernard saw it and began to shout hysterically,

"YOUR DOG HAS EATEN MY CAT!!"

"No, no," Freddie replied in a soothing tone. "I'm sure there's another explanation."

"I don't think so. He's always hated Otto and now he's killed him. He has taken the bow tie as a trophy."

The Inspector was frowning a little. "Flapjack, you need to show us where you found this," he said.

Flapjack gave a short bark as if to say, *Come on then!* and set off toward the cherry trees.

"The scene of the crime," Bernard uttered dramatically. "I can hardly bear to look."

CHAPTER NINE

Flapjack led them along under the cherry trees to the farthest tree. They could hear a terrible noise of birds squawking—something was clearly going on.

"The birds must be gathering around his corpse like vultures," Bernard cried.

"I don't think so," the Inspector replied, rolling his eyes, and sure enough, when they reached the tree where all the kerfuffle was coming from and looked up, there was Otto alive and well.

He was hauling himself up to a bird's nest, bit by bit, like a mountaineer, using his claws like grappling hooks, while the poor mother and father bird squawked at him in horror.

"Oh, thank goodness, he's alive!" Bernard cried. And then quickly added, "Flapjack must have chased him up there."

"The evidence does not suggest that," the Inspector said drily. "Now let's get him down before he reaches the nest."

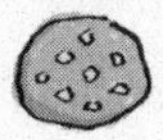

A ladder was fetched.

"Bernard, you had better go up and get him. He'll scratch anyone else to pieces," the Inspector said.

"Me? Oh no, I'm sorry, I can't. I am terribly afraid of heights," Bernard stuttered.

"I'll go," said Freddie calmly.

"You're braver than me, Freddie," the Inspector said.

Poor Freddie! Otto was so angry that he had been stopped from reaching the nest that he was a ball of spitting fury, with his ears pinned back and making that moaning noise like something stuck in the vacuum that cats make when they're cross. He scratched poor Freddie, several times.

"You must have been holding him the wrong way," Bernard said ungraciously when they reached the ground.

"There you go, Otto," Freddie said to the cat as he handed him over.

"Well, you and Flapjack are heroes," the Inspector said. "Don't you agree, Bernard?"

"I suppose so," said Bernard reluctantly, and managed to say a stammering thank you.

Posy came over.

"Oh, you found him, I'm so pleased," she said. "If only Flapjack could find Cookie for me," she added sadly.

Everyone congratulated Flapjack and it was decided that he deserved a sausage roll. So Amira went over to the picnic table to fetch him one, just as a policeman jogged over to them,

clutching an envelope.

"The fingerprint results are in, sir, from the cake theft outside Van de Lune's Hotel," he said breathlessly to Inspector Brown and handed him the envelope.

Bernard went very hot and sweaty and his heart began to beat wildly. All he could think about was running away before they found out it was him. "Er . . . I must be going," he stammered.

"Oh no, wait," the Inspector said. "Aren't you interested to see who stole Freddie's cakes?"

Bernard swallowed hard, unable to breathe, let alone think what to reply. He began to gasp like a fish out of water.

"You never know, the results might help find Cookie," Freddie said.

Posy's face brightened and they watched intently as the Inspector opened the envelope and read the result.

A wave of blind panic swept over Bernard as he heard the Inspector say, "So the results are . . ."

And Bernard found himself shouting,

"IT WAS ME! I STOLE THE CAKES!"

There was a long stunned silence as everyone turned and stared at him.

"You stole my cakes?" Freddie asked, looking bewildered.

"Yes," Bernard replied, looking shamefaced. He mopped his sweaty forehead with his spotty handkerchief.

"But why didn't you just come into the shop and buy some?" Freddie asked.

"Because I . . . I . . ." Bernard stammered. "I was too embarrassed," he replied eventually. "It was wrong of me and I'm s . . . s . . . sorry," he managed to say, staring at the floor.

"Did you take Cookie too?" Posy asked, looking at Bernard with new, horrified eyes.

"No, no, absolutely not," Bernard replied. "I swear I would never do such a thing."

There was another pause.

"Well I was about to say that the

results were inconclusive," the Inspector said. "But that clearly doesn't matter now. Bernard, I am arresting you for cake theft."

Bernard went milk white and his eyes filled with tears.

"But I can't go to jail! What will become of poor Otto?" he wailed. "It's not his fault."

Despite everything, Freddie felt sorry for Bernard. He took the Inspector to one side.

"Is it really necessary for him to be arrested?" Freddie asked him. "Couldn't you just give him a warning?"

The Inspector thought for a moment and then replied, "Well, I suppose so. They were your cakes that he stole, so if it's OK with you, it is with me."

They rejoined the others and the

Inspector said, in a very stern voice, "Bernard, what you did was very wrong. Do you promise never to steal anything again?" Bernard stopped wailing and his face perked up.

"Oh yes, absolutely," he replied quickly. "I swear on Otto's life."

"Are you happy with that, Freddie?" the Inspector asked.

"I am," Freddie replied.

"Bernard, you are free to go," the Inspector announced.

"Thank you so very, very much," Bernard gushed, worried that they would change their minds. "I promise I will never do anything bad again. Now," he went on, mopping his brow with his handkerchief, "I think Otto and I had better go and have a cup of tea and sit down."

Just as Bernard was about to walk away a thought occurred to him. "Freddie, please could I ask you one more small favor? Please, please could you not mention this to Amira?"

Freddie smiled. "OK, Bernard," he replied.

CHAPTER TEN

Amira returned with Dr. Wells and not one but two sausage rolls. Flapjack gave a yelp of delight and disappeared under a table with them.

"Did you ever get to the bottom of where Flapjack kept disappearing to?" Dr. Wells asked Freddie.

"No," Freddie said. "We tried following him like you suggested, but we lost him. So it remains a mystery."

"Perhaps he's stopped now."

"Yes, I suppose so," Freddie said and he bent down under the table to give Flapjack a pat. But Flapjack wasn't there.

"Oh no! Not again!" Freddie exclaimed.

"Don't worry," Dr. Wells said. "Let's go and look for him. He won't have gone far."

They set off in different directions. Word spread and Amira, Posy, Sophie, Noah, and the Inspector all joined in the hunt.

Oh, Flapjack, where have you gone? Freddie thought, beginning to feel concerned. But then there was a shout from Sophie over by the carousel and they all headed there.

"I've found him," Sophie said, when Freddie and the others reached her.

“Where is he?” Freddie asked, looking puzzled.

“I’ll show you, but everyone needs to be quiet,” Sophie replied and led them around the far side of the carousel.

“Look,” she said, bending down.

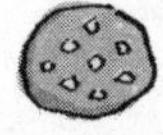

There was a gap of a couple of feet underneath the carousel and there was Flapjack with . . . Cookie. She was snuggled up in a nest of old sacks eating the sausage roll, while Flapjack lay next to her. And then the biggest surprise of all! Lying asleep beside her were one, two, three, four, five tiny kittens . . .

Everyone gasped and said things like:

“Oh my goodness!”

“How amazing!”

“Wow!”

"Did you even know Cookie was pregnant?" the Inspector asked.

Posy, who was laughing and crying at the same time, managed to say, "No, I had no idea."

"So Cookie wasn't stolen, she ran away," the Inspector said.

"I guess she didn't want her kittens to be TV stars," Noah said.

"And it looks as if Flapjack has been looking after them all," added Sophie.

"So that's why he kept stealing food—it was for Cookie," Freddie said. He bent down and stroked Flapjack. "I'm sorry I thought you were just being naughty."

"He's an exceptionally good dog," the Inspector said.

"Shall I take a look at Cookie and the kittens, Posy? Just to check that they're OK?" Dr. Wells offered.

“Yes please,” replied Posy.

After a few minutes, he said, “Five very sweet, healthy kittens and Cookie is doing very well too, thanks to Flapjack. Shall we take them back to the hotel?”

Freddie fetched one of the large boxes that the cakes had been packed in and Posy and Dr. Wells carefully transferred the kittens into it. Posy carried Cookie who, judging by the thunderous purring, was very pleased to see her, and Dr. Wells carried the kittens.

"Bernard, could you give us a lift in your very fine motorcar?" he asked, and they all sped off to Van de Lune's Hotel.

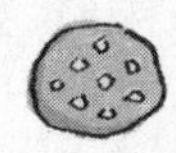

"Well wasn't that lovely?" Amira said later, as she and Freddie helped Noah clear up. The sun was setting over Belville, casting a lovely golden light over the park. The Belville Blasters had played their final encore and the last few picnickers were packing up and making their way home.

"It was the perfect end to a perfect day," Freddie replied happily.

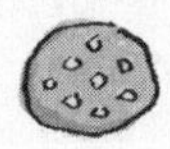

Well, Flapjack turned out to be a total star, didn't he? And he had a very good week afterward because, not only was Freddie being incredibly nice to him, but also:

On Monday Sophie made a bumper crop of sausage rolls all for him.

On Tuesday Posy gave him a magnificent new collar that said HERO on it.

On Wednesday there was a special ceremony at the police station, where Flapjack was awarded a medal by Inspector Brown for OUTSTANDING SERVICE.

On Thursday there was a big article about him in the *Belville News*, which meant that everyone who came in the shop made a fuss of him and that inevitably led to . . . you guessed it . . . more sausage rolls.

And then on Friday, which was the last one of the month, the most amazing showstopper cake appeared in the bakery window of Cookie and her kittens with Flapjack looking over them. Posy loved the cake so much that she paid a huge amount of money for it, which, along with the money raised by the picnic, paid for the carousel to be repaired. Hurrah!

Spring turned to summer and Posy, Cookie, and the kittens went back to their normal life with no TV cameras or bossy young men with clipboards (but you might be interested to hear that Hubert was soon busy with a TV series all about the world's funniest parrot). Sophie went off to the École Pâtissier in Paris, which was a big adventure for her. Bernard presented Amira with many more bunches of flowers. And Freddie . . . well, he kept on baking because that's what he loves to do.

Harriet Whitehorn grew up in London where she still lives with her family. She is the author of numerous books for young readers, and has been nominated for several awards, including the Waterstones Children's Book Prize.

Alex G. Griffiths is an illustrator specializing in children's picture books and character design. The majority of his work is done by hand, using a combination of pen-and-ink line work and brush textures in a messy way to create a natural style of illustration.

GLOSSARY

BAKE to bake food is to cook it in an oven, especially bread or cakes

BATTER a mixture of flour, eggs, and milk beaten together and used to make pancakes and baked goods

BEAT to beat a cooking mixture is to stir it quickly so that it becomes thicker

BISCUIT a hard, crunchy cookie

BOIL to boil a liquid is to heat it until it starts to bubble

BRIOCHE a light sweet bread typically in the form of a small round roll

BUTTERCREAM a soft mixture of butter and powdered sugar used as a filling or topping for a cake

CAKE sweet food made from a baked mixture of flour, eggs, fat, and sugar

CROISSANT a crescent-shaped roll made from rich pastry

DOUGH a thick mixture of flour and water used for making bread or pastry

ÉCLAIR a finger-shaped cake of pastry with a cream filling

FONDANT ICING a thick icing made from water and sugar

GATEAU a rich cream cake